HWS Publishing

ISBN 978-0-9815285-2-6
ISBN 0-9815285-2-X

December 2008

This book is dedicated
to our many friends from
Canada and around the globe
who make the long journey.

One day, Lois the Duck came home with some great news for her husband. "Lewis, I am so excited. My office is sending me on a special project and you'll never guess where I'm going…Canada! I've never been there before."

"Oh honey, how wonderful," Lewis said. "How long will you be gone?"

"I'll be gone a whole week," Lois said. "Lisa and Lance both have summer day camp that week, so you'll need to pick them up by 5:30 every night."

Lewis started thinking. He'd never been to Canada either. "Why don't we make it a family vacation? The kids and I could fly up after your business is finished!"

"Why Lewis, that's a great idea," she said. "We're all due a vacation. School is out – it's the perfect time."

"Don't worry honey; I'll take care of everything," Lewis said.

S oon it was time for Lois to fly, so Lewis and the kids started planning the family's trip. He told Lisa and Lance, "We'll need passports – Canada is a different country and we'll have to cross the border. And, we'll need to figure out what we want to do."

L ewis and his kids found many great things to do and some interesting facts.

CANADA'S TEN PROVINCES AND THREE TERRITORIES

- ALBERTA
- BRITISH COLUMBIA
- MANITOBA
- NEW BRUNSWICK
- NEWFOUNDLAND/ LABRADOR
- NORTHWEST TERRITORIES
- NOVA SCOTIA
- NUNAVUT
- ONTARIO
- PRINCE EDWARD ISLAND
- QUEBEC
- SASKATCHEWAN
- YUKON TERRITORY

CANADA DAY!

Canada became a Country on July 1, 1867

Canada is on t
North America
largest country

NORTH AMERICA

CAN

The big day to leave finally came – they had their bags packed and their passports under their wings. They took off!

As soon as they landed at the Canadian border they got in line at customs. Lewis and his brood showed their passports to the agent and told him they were on a family vacation. "Have fun," said the agent as he smiled and stamped their passports.

Soon they got to their favourite hotel and the kids saw their mom – "Mom, Mom!" they screamed. Lewis gave Lois a big hug and a kiss and said, "We missed you! How was your week?" "Just ducky!" she said, "It couldn't have been better and now I get to have fun and explore with my favourite little wingers!"

And off they flew. What a great week they had flying all over Canada. And what great experiences they had.

The family got a duck's eye view of the Toronto skyline from atop one of the world's tallest free-standing structures, the CN Tower.

T hey got to know Canadian history at Parliament Hill

in the capital city of Ottawa.

They took in the breathtaking views of Niagara Falls.

And went hiking and biking in the Laurentian Mountains.

LAURENTIDES

← THE LAURENTIAN MOUNTAINS

Lisa ordered en francais when the family dined at a fancy restaurant in Montreal, Quebec.

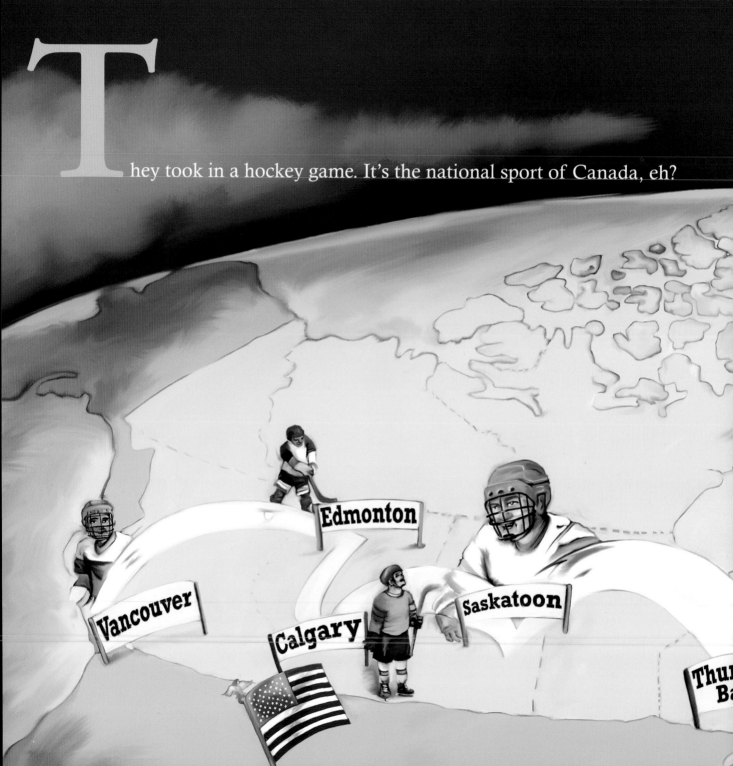

They took in a hockey game. It's the national sport of Canada, eh?

They even met a real Royal Canadian Mounted Policeman –

an officer from the national police force.

At Wood Buffalo National Park in Alberta, they saw the home of the world's largest bison herd and the only nesting site of the endangered whooping crane.

On the last day of their trip, they went orca watching off the coast of British Columbia.

"What a great week!" Lewis said. "Honey, we've had a blast, but it's time to go home."

"I know Lewis," Lois said. "I've been gone for over two weeks, but it's been quite an adventure." So they packed up, said goodbye to their friends at the hotel and flew home. Lewis and his family were glad to land back at home...but they sure did miss Canada.

"Well," thought Lewis, "There's always next year."

Author Bio:
Bill Duncan lives in Memphis, Tennessee,
with his wife Julie and son Christian.
Lewis The Duck and His Long Trip was his first book.

Artist Bio:
Greg Cravens is the creator of the syndicated cartoon,
The Buckets and *Lewis The Duck and His Long Trip*.
He enjoys spending time with his wife Paula
and sons Gideon and Cory.

The Story of Lewis

Our guests often ask, "Why the duck?
Who is he and what does a duck have to do with Homewood Suites?"

Homewood Suites chose a duck because it symbolizes versatility and adaptability.
Ducks are comfortable in air, in water, and on land. They migrate long
distances over extended periods. And their ability to adapt and thrive in
a variety of places represents our goal in the travel and hospitality industry – to
serve guests with resourcefulness and flexibility.

We chose a wood duck, considered one of the most beautiful creatures in
nature. And we've given him a name – Lewis. By naming Lewis and bringing
him to life, we've created a visual representation of a unique brand that caters
to those who want the comforts of home when on the road for a few days
or more. And, with Lewis to guide us, there is no doubt that we will meet our
guests' individual needs for comfort, flexibility and convenience.

HOMEWOOD
SUITES
—— Hilton ——